E JULIAN

First published in the United States, Great Britain, Canada, Australia, and
New Zealand in 2018 by NorthSouth Books, Inc., an imprint of
NordSüd Verlag AG, CH-8050 Zürich, Switzerland.

Distributed in the United States by NorthSouth Books, Inc., New York 10016.
Library of Congress Cataloging-in-Publication Data is available.
ISBN: 978-0-7358-4306-6 (trade edition)
1 3 5 7 9 • 10 8 6 4 2

Printed in Germany by Grafisches Centrum Cuno GmbH & Co. KG, 2017.

www.northsouth.com

SLOPPY

Takes the Plunge

By Sean Julian

North
South

"Are you having fun, Sloppy?"
Dewdrop asked.

"Jumping in puddles and
getting muddy is always fun,"
Sloppy replied.

"It's not as much fun as having a big hug though."

"I can't hug you," said Dewdrop.

"Why not?"

"Because you're all mucky."

"Only
a little bit,"
Sloppy moaned.

"You're covered in mud,"
said Dewdrop.

"I think you need to have a bath!"

"Tree dragons don't take baths!
Being mucky is what being a tree dragon
is all about."

"You've never had a bath?"

"Never,"
said Sloppy proudly.

"Well it's about time you did!" said Dewdrop.
"You never know; you might enjoy it."

"I won't,"
Sloppy replied.

Dewdrop smiled.
"How would you know
if you've never
tried it?"

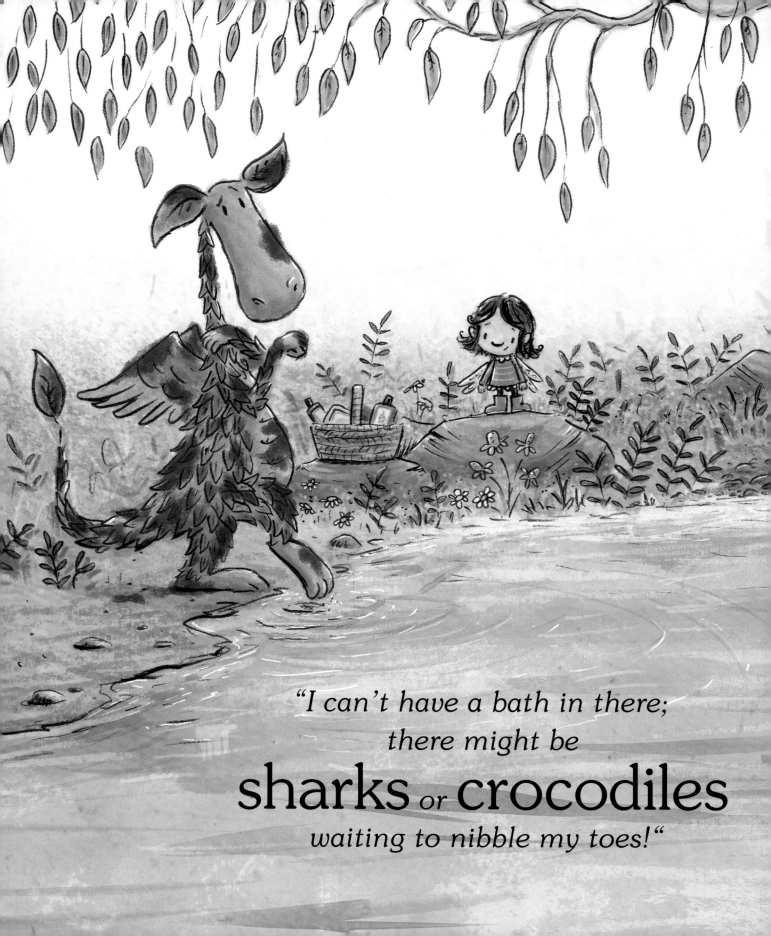

"I can't have a bath in there;
there might be

sharks *or* crocodiles

waiting to nibble my toes!"

"There are only fish in this pond. I'm sure they'll quickly swim away when you get in," Dewdrop pointed out.

"Looks like you're not the only one afraid of taking their first bath," said Dewdrop.

The little ducklings were scared and would not follow their mommy into the water.

Quack!
(Sharks!) Quack!
(Crocodiles!)

"I'm sure there's nothing to be afraid of,"
said Sloppy.

"What if I go first to show you that it's all safe?"

Sloppy was still a little afraid, so he checked the pool for anything that might want to nibble his toes and then bravely . . .

... took his first ever bath.

And when they saw Sloppy being brave, the ducklings, one by one, took their first ever bath too.

Sloppy found getting clean was nearly as much fun as getting muddy.

When all the mud was washed away,
Sloppy had to admit that he felt . . .

AMAZING!

"Well done, Sloppy! You were very brave, and you helped the ducklings find their courage."

"I was very brave, wasn't I?" Sloppy smiled.

Dewdrop gave her newly clean
friend a big hug. . . .

Sloppy gave Dewdrop a
great big gooey **lick**.

"YUCK!"

"I think it's my turn to have a bath," said Dewdrop.

"Can I have a bath too?" Sloppy asked.

"But you're not mucky," Dewdrop replied.

"Not Yet!"

said Sloppy . . .

... before jumping into the biggest puddle of mud he could find.